PENGUIN'S PARTY
PROBLEMS

Alice Horn

This book belongs to

....

Every year Papa Penguin
was given the task
of planning the family
birthday celebrations.
But things didn't always
turn out perfectly . . .

One morning, Papa Penguin was just settling down
to enjoy a nice cup of tea when Daddy Penguin
called out, "It really isn't long until Baby Penguin's
birthday — is everything sorted for the party?"

BABY
PENGUIN'S
BIRTHDAY

This year he was going to make
sure it was the greatest
birthday party ever, and he knew
he couldn't do it alone!

He would need the help
of his best friends!

Lion and Tortoise were
known for their silly jokes . . .

Orangutan and Giraffe for
their wild dance moves . . .

and Crocodile and Anteater
were always up for a laugh!

Hey, it's Baby Penguin's birthday soon and I can't have a repeat of last year. I need your help to make this year special.

Of course Penguin! We're always here to help! What do you need us to do?

We need food, drinks, decorations, party games and music!

I can definitely sort out the music for you, Penguin.

You know I'm always great with party games! Leave it with me.

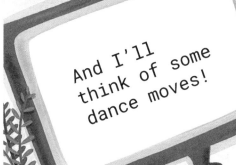
And I'll think of some dance moves!

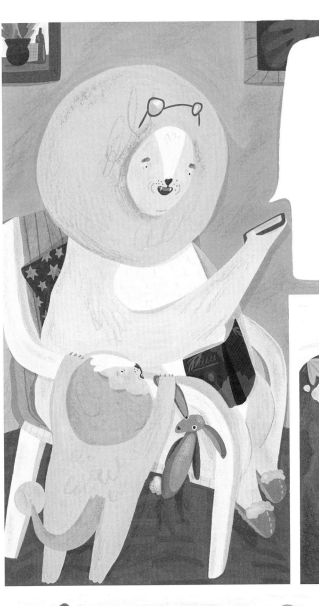

I'd love to help with the decorations! I'll get the balloons, streamers and party poppers.

And I can get the plates, cups and paper straws!

I can do the food! I know that's one thing I'll be good at!

I suppose that leaves me with drinks!

Thanks for your help everyone! You truly are the best. I'll head to the supermarket tomorrow!

The next day when Penguin set off on his journey to the supermarket, he was unsure of what to buy . . .

but when he got there, he knew exactly what to get!

"FISH!"

"Everyone loves fish!"

When Penguin got home,
he messaged everyone
to let them know about
their delicious food.

Great news everyone!
I got us fish for
Baby Penguin's party! :)

Penguin . . .
Sorry I forgot to say –
I only eat leaves!

Amazing, Penguin!
I absolutely
LOVE fish.

Oh, fish sticks!
Sorry, Giraffe,
how could I forget?

So Penguin grabbed his
trolley and headed back to
the supermarket.

Why would
anyone
want to
eat this?!

HERBIVORE

Penguin, feeling pretty confident he'd got everything he needed for the party, started to put away the shopping in the kitchen. But then his phone beeped . . .

Hi Penguin, sorry I forgot to say earlier but I can only eat ants!

No problem, Anteater. I'll get you some.

So off Penguin went, back to the supermarket . . .

again.

"What a peculiar thing
to want to eat!"
Penguin thought
to himself.

INSECTIVORE

Confused,
and now a little itchy,
Penguin headed home.

Back home, Penguin started
to unload the ants
when a message popped up
on his phone . . .

Penguin, forgive me
pal, but I actually
only eat fruit. My
favourite is durian.
It's the one that
smells a bit cheesy!

Orangutan!
Not my thing but
never mind, I'll
see what I can find.

So off went poor Penguin,
back to the supermarket . . .

AGAIN!

"Surely this must be everything!"
Penguin thought.
"But wait a second, what's that?"

Penguin, good news is I've sorted out all the decorations. I'll send them over to you. Bad news is that I forgot to mention I only eat meat.

Oh Lion . . .

Ahhhhh, not AGAIN!

Back in the supermarket,
Penguin picked out some bits for Lion
and then hurried on home.

Surrounded by all the food from his shopping trips, Penguin was quite sure he had everything now.

But then . . .

Hi Penguin, just a quick one to say my wife's got me on a new vegan diet. I don't really fancy Orangutan's cheesy fruit, so could you get me some vegetables?

Penguin, being the kind-hearted type, didn't hesitate to grab his trolley . . .

... as he headed back
to the supermarket
for the last time.

Finally Penguin was back home and the supermarket was a distant memory.

But what on earth was Penguin going to make for the party with all this?!

Penguin spent the night tossing and turning trying to think of what he could make with all these different foods.

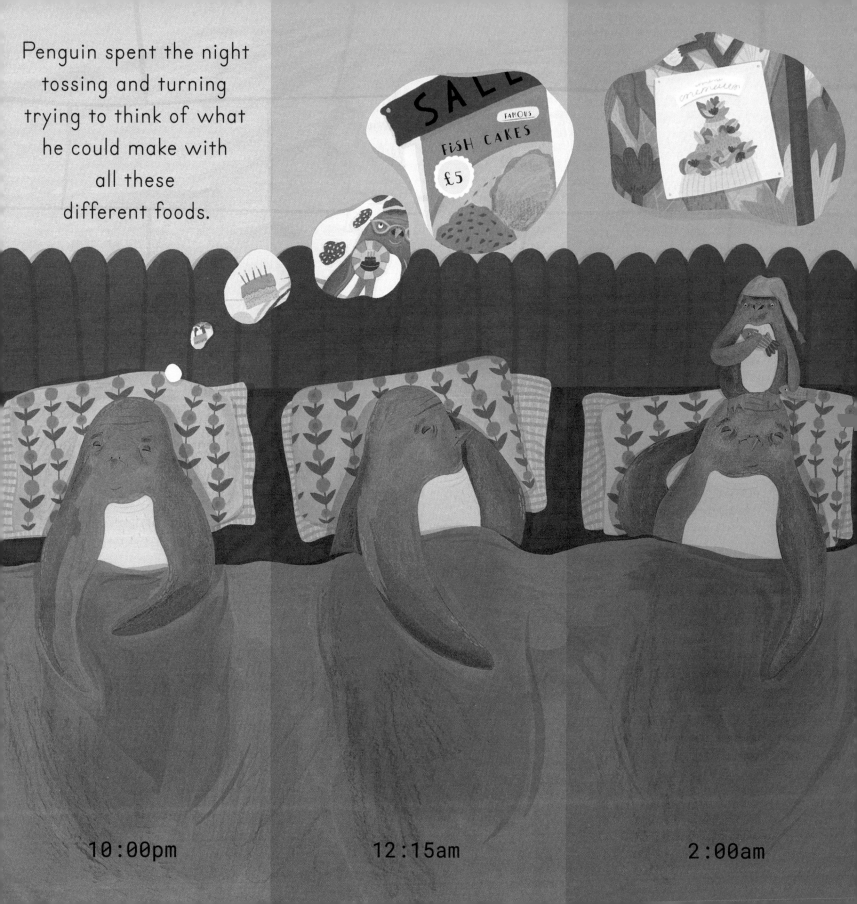

10:00pm

12:15am

2:00am

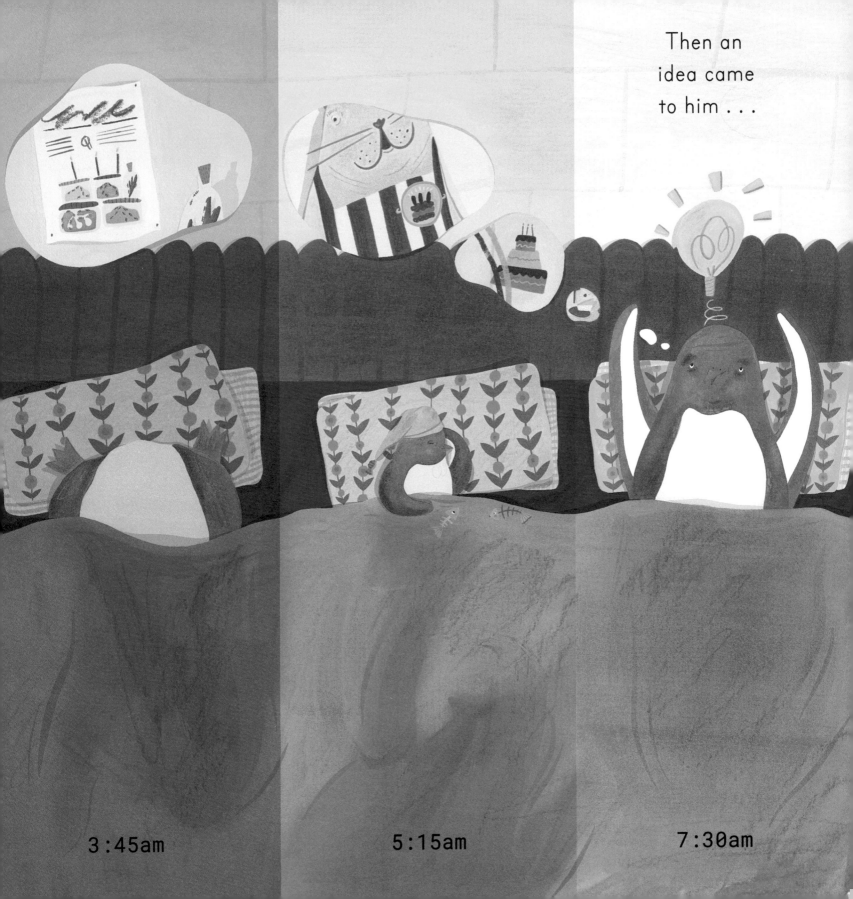

Then an
idea came
to him . . .

3:45am

5:15am

7:30am

"I'll make a CAKE!"

"Of course,
every birthday party
needs a cake!
Everyone loves cake!"

Now the cake was in the oven, Penguin finally had a chance to put up all the decorations Lion had sent over.

Soon enough there was a knock on the door!

"They're here!"

"HAPPY BIRTHDAY BABY PENGUIN!"

When everyone saw the cake,
they couldn't believe their eyes.
"This is genius, Penguin!
It has all our favourite things!"
everyone cheered.
Baby Penguin's birthday party
was the best yet!

But where had
Penguin got to?

To my parents, Tom, and Jimmy,
for being the greatest people in my life.
Thank you for constant support . . .
even when I'm stressed like Penguin.

First published 2021 by order of the Tate Trustees
by Tate Publishing, a division of Tate Enterprises Ltd,
Millbank, London SW1P 4RG
www.tate.org.uk/publishing

A catalogue record for this book is available from the British Library

ISBN 978 1 84976 764 4

Distributed in the United States and Canada by ABRAMS, New York
Library of Congress Control Number applied for

Colour reproduction by Evergreen Colour Management Ltd
Printed and bound in China by C&C Offset Printing Co., Ltd